A Boy, A Girl
& The Fox

J.R LEE

CONTENTS

ACKNOWLEDGMENTS

I am grateful for the help, support and feedback provided by my family and friends to better improve this book.

I would also like to mention that the cover of the book was done using Canva.

Finally, I would like to note that this website had enabled me to learn more about the culture and history of Fushimi Inari Taisha.
お稲荷さんへようこそ　参拝音声ガイド. 伏見稲荷神社. (n.d.)
http://fushimiinari.jp/en/index.html

CHAPTER 1:
"TAKASHI ARIMA"

"Dreams and goals, huh? What do they even mean to me?" I pondered as I stared at the blank preference form in my hand. Scenes of what had happened in the classroom last week appeared in my mind.

"Has everyone received a copy of the preference form?" asked the teacher. The class replied with a unanimous: "Yes!"

"Assuming that all of you pass, you will be graduating, and your next step is to decide on a future path to take. Some of you here may be planning to further your studies at university, while others may enter vocational schools or even start working. The form in front of you helps me to better guide you to your desired path. Please fill up the form and submit it back to me after the spring break in three months."

Two years have flown by since I lost the most precious part of myself. Ever since then, a dark cloud has been cast over my life, ironically like the day that it happened. A tear unknowingly rolled down my cheeks.

"What should I do after high school?" I mused, staring at the ceiling under my duvet. Frustration built within me. Eventually, I did what I always did to problems I could not solve, procrastinate. I pulled the covers over my head and decided to let the tomorrow-me deal with it.

"Beep! Beep!" the alarm clock rang. I put a pillow on my head to muffle the sound, but it kept getting louder and louder. Half conscious, I wriggled my arm free and fumbled for the clock that was beeping relentlessly. Accidentally, I knocked it off the table, further from me. I got up irritated, and tromped over to the clock, cussing at it silently. "What a great day." I headed to the shower to wash up and prepared a bento before heading to the train station to commute to school. In Japan, the most common mode of transportation is by rail. Like every other day, the oshidas were hard at work, cramming more passengers onto the train. I barely managed to squeeze into one. This was a hassle I had to deal with daily. "I can't wait for this to end!" I thought to myself. My high school was located right beside the train station. Hence, it was common to see people from my school on the train.

Stop after stop passed, and I soon arrived at my stop. "Finally! I'm out of that hell hole!" I thought to myself. I proceeded to head to school. Classes began just as I reached. It was the usual drone of the teacher's voice, punctured by the occasional chatter and clicking of pens. Despite my ambivalence towards school, I knew it was something I had to deal with, as having a basic level of education is necessary for survival in a highly competitive country like Japan. "I cannot wait for recess!" I thought to myself. I looked at the clock, and it was 11.55am, just five minutes more. "Come on! Just end already!" I mumbled to myself. The five minutes felt like an eternity.

Finally, it was recess. The class rose to attention as the teacher dismissed them over the bell. The mood in the classroom changed from dead silence to a vibrant and lively atmosphere. Groups of three to five people started to form. Some of these clusters proceeded to the cafeteria for lunch, while others remained in class to continue their chattering. Just like every other day, I chose to be alone, or so that was what I told myself. I could not remember when I started being alone or if it had always been this way, but the peace and quiet were something I was used to. I headed to my usual corner to have my lunch while watching gaming streams and reading up on the new manga released.

But good times are often short, and soon I had to head back to class for lessons. I had another three hours of lessons before the day came to an end. I sat through one class after another, and soon the day came to an end. I went to the school library to complete my homework for the day before heading back home after buying dinner at the convenience stall near my apartment.

"I'm back!" I called out. There was nothing but silence that greeted me. The silence reminded me that I was living alone. I dragged my feet to my room and threw my bag on my bed. I proceeded to turn on my computer and started to play video games while eating dinner. I continued playing till my eyelids were heavy enough to let me drift off to sleep.

This was a typical day of my school life. My days blended together with no distinction or purpose. I would wake up, shower and head to school. After classes had ended, I would head to the library and then head home, only to lose myself in video games till I was exhausted enough to sleep.

This was until I met her…

CHAPTER 2:
THE SECRET

An announcement was made through the hospital public address system, "Patient Takashi Arima, please proceed to the pharmacy to collect your medication. Thank you."

Upon hearing the announcement, I proceeded to the pharmacy to collect my medication.

When I arrived, I saw a nurse running across the hallway while calling upon a patient: "Mori-san! Mori-san! Please wait! You left without your medication!" A young teenager with blonde hair turned around in response to the call. I noticed she was my high school classmate, Mori Hikari. She was one of the more popular and outgoing girls in the class. She had a certain charisma which was able to bring people together. Contrary to her, I was an introvert who preferred spending my days alone and did not have any friends. We were worlds apart.

Hikari replied to the nurse: "Oh! Sorry for the trouble. Thanks for bringing my medication to me." The nurse responded: "No worries! Do remember to take the medication on time to ensure the effectiveness of the treatment!" As the nurse passed the medication to Hikari, I caught a glimpse of the name of the medicine: Sorafenib.

"That name sounds familiar?" I pondered to myself. "Sorafenib…? Wait! Isn't that the drug used to treat liver cancer? Does Hikari have liver cancer?" I was aware of the Sorafenib drug as I had chanced upon this term in one of the books I read in the library. "It would be better to leave before she sees me here!"

As I was about to make a move, the pharmacist at the counter called upon my name: "Mr Takashi, your medication is ready." From the corner of my eyes, I felt her gaze on me.

After collecting my medication, I spotted Hikari waiting at the corner. I avoided eye contact with her and attempted to walk away without her noticing. However, she walked in front of me to block my path.

"So Arima, you know my condition, don't you?" She asked.

"I saw the nurse handing you some medication. That is all! I know nothing about your liver cancer condition!" I accidentally blurted. Realising that I had unintentionally revealed to Hikari my awareness of her condition, I was worried that this would result in a troublesome situation. Hence, I reassured her that she did not have to worry about me spreading her condition as there was no one in class I communicated with.

Her response was solemn. "I am dying of liver cancer, and I have only a few months left to live." As she was neither someone I was close to nor someone I cared about, I was indifferent to the news and responded by saying: "Ok. Live your remaining months the way you want it to be!" and proceeded to leave. Hikari burst into laughter: "Haha! Out of all the people who were aware of my condition, you are the first who showed no concern at all! Anyways, since you know about my condition, I will stalk you starting from today to ensure that you refrain from telling any of our classmates about my condition." I retorted: "Suit yourself!" and we went our separate ways.

The next day, as usual, I proceeded to the library after school. Every student in the high school was required to participate in club activities after school. As I was an introvert and did not like communicating with others, I chose to join the reading club, which was essentially playing the role of a librarian. Hence, I would spend most of my time after school at the school library. I was informed by the teacher-in-charge of the club earlier that day that there was a new member who would be joining the club today. To my surprise, that new member was Hikari. She cheekily smiled and greeted me: "Hi Arima! Please show me the ropes."

Arranging the books in alphabetical order was one of the duties as part of the reading club. So, I proceeded to show her the appropriate way to arrange the books on the shelves. While "we" – mainly I –

were arranging the books on the bookshelves, she kept chattering to me about her day, what she had for lunch, her favourite drama etc. I tried hard to tune her voice out but to no avail. Sensing a stare or two, I sighed and whispered to her: "We are in a library! What do you want? I am certain you did not join this club because you are interested in it."

"I told you yesterday, didn't I? I am stalking you from now on since you know my secret."

"You do not have to worry about me revealing your secret. In fact, I could not care less. Can you just leave me alone?"

She smiled mischievously. "Sure! But only if you promise to fulfil three wishes on my bucket list." Slightly taken aback, I responded: "Why should I?"

Her joy turned into dejection. "My family are the only ones aware of my condition. But ever since they knew about my condition, they started to treat me differently, with utmost care and caution. That is not how I want to spend my remaining days on this earth! I would like to live my remaining days normally without being treated differently, but I know it is hard for them. I cannot let my friends know about my condition. Knowing them, they would treat me like how my parents are treating me now."

Her voice quickly became shaky. "Arima, you were the only one who treated me the same despite knowing my condition. Only with you, I can truly be myself. There is not anyone else I can depend on but you, Arima!" With tears welling in her eyes, she leaned forward and whispered in my ear: "You wouldn't be so heartless towards a dying classmate, would you…" Her voice trailed off into silence. A tinge of pity gripped my conscience.

"Fine! I will fulfil your wishes if it is not something beyond me."

Hikari stretched out her right pinky towards me and said: "Let's do a pinky promise, so that you won't back out halfway!" I stretched my right pinky and interlock it with Hikari's.

"Hooray! Mission accomplished!" Hikari shouted in joy and grabbed me by my arm. A few loud "Shhh!" punctured our conversation while Hikari quietly mumbled a "Sorry!" She then grabbed my phone from my pocket and keyed in her number.

And so, I began fulfilling her three wishes.

CHAPTER 3:
THE FIRST WISH

On Saturday that weekend, I received a text from Hikari: "Hey Arima! It's me! Let's meet up at the café near school! See you there! I am not leaving till I see you!" Her text ended off with a cheeky face emoji. My usual routine would be cramping up in my room playing games or reading the weekly manga magazine. I was not in the mood to step out of my house, let alone my bedroom. However, recalling my promise to Hikari, I reluctantly dragged my feet out of the house.

I stepped outside my house and felt the blazing heat pounding on my back. The glare of the radiant sun blinded my eyes. Throughout the journey to the café, I was constantly grumbling: "Why the heck did I even agree to this?" My frustrated monologue continued until I arrived in front of the café.

As I stepped into the café, the doorbell rang. The staff of the café greeted me warmly and I nodded back politely. I proceeded to scan the surroundings of the café. Hikari was nowhere to be found. "I can't believe she is late!" I grunted. Out of the blue, I felt a tap on my right shoulder. I turned around to see if it was Hikari, but there was no one there. Then from my left, Hikari appeared out of nowhere and shouted: "Surprise!"

"So why do you want to meet today?" I replied with a straight face. She whined: "Humph! You're no fun! Anyways, I am here to discuss the first wish I have on my bucket list."

"And what would that first wish on your bucket list be?" I droned. She ignored my lack of enthusiasm and cheerfully responded: "My first wish is to go on a cosplay date at the upcoming anime festival!"

"Forget it, you can go by yourself."

"But I want you to come with me!"

"I'll have to think about it," I shrugged.

Hikari pouted and made doe eyes at me. I begrudgingly relented as we were attracting stares from other customers around us.

"However, I will not dress up, I'll only accompany you there."

"That's not fair! It wouldn't be a date like that!" Hikari whined.

"Fine, you're so annoying, what do you have in mind?"

She chuckled: "I'll dress as Princess Peach, and you can be Toad!"

"The mushroom guy? No way! He's short and ugly!"

"Exactly! You wouldn't even have to dress up! You're already short and ugly!" Hikari teased.

"I'm taller than you short stuff," I stood up from my seat and was about to leave the cafe. At that instant, Hikari grabbed me by the arm and hugged it tightly.

"Fine, I'm sorry! Will you still go with me?"

"Fine" I huffed.

Hikari exclaimed in joy: "Woohoo! We are going on a cosplay date together!" Subsequently, we left the café, and we began our preparation for the anime fest, which was in a month.

The following week, Hikari texted me her house address to meet up to discuss the costume we would be wearing. The address given by Hikari was from a wealthy neighbourhood in Tokyo. It took some time to locate the exact place. After much searching, I finally arrived at the stated address. A luxurious 19th-century-style mansion loomed over me.

"I guess this should be it!" I thought to myself. I apprehensively rang the doorbell, afraid that I was at the wrong place. A low, distinctly male voice echoed through the intercom: "May I know who you might be looking for?" I mumbled nervously: "I… I am looking for Hikari. She invited me over here today." The male over the intercom replied: "Oh! You must be Arima! Miss Hikari is expecting you!" The massive gates of the mansion swung open; a butler was at the ready to guide me into the residence.

As I entered the mansion, I was impressed by what I saw. The mansion exuded grandeur with its tall ceilings, large windows, and an exquisite crystal chandelier hung from the high ceilings. The butler directed me to the first left room on the second floor, where Hikari was waiting for me in her bedroom. I thanked the butler and headed to the second floor.

I gently knocked on the bedroom door. "Hikari! Arima here! Can I come in?" Hikari replied: "Come in!"

Pushing open the door, I was greeted by an angelic presence. Hikari was wearing a floor-length French pink dress with a layer of reddish-pink at the hem of the dress. The dress had puff sleeves and an up-turn collar design. The dress was accompanied by a blue gem brooch set in gold and a tiara with a pink diamond set in the middle. The dress was well fitted, and it contoured her body perfectly. It brought out every inch of her beauty.

I stared at her, suddenly lost for words. "Hey... Hey! Why are you staring so much!" She blushed in embarrassment. I snapped back to reality and stuttered an apology.

"It's fine! Anyways, how do I look in my cosplay outfit?"

"You look uh…beautiful!"

"You aren't suddenly shy just because of this right?" Hikari smirked

"That tiara looks really expensive, are you sure you're wearing that out?" I tried to divert the conversation.

Luckily, she took the bait.

"It's really shiny, I'll get a lot of looks with it!"

"What if you lose it? We'll be walking around all day too. You might drop it."

"Hmm, I guess I could go with something less flashy."

"Alright, go change, I'll wait here for you."

Hikari wagged her finger in disapproval and pointed towards a closet by the side of the room: "No no, you need to go change too, your outfit is over there, go try it on!"

Wow… it's really an outfit of a mushroom. I thought I had managed to get away from having to be in costume by not preparing anything.

After changing, I stared at the body-length

mirror and felt a little insecure, my costume was drab, compared to Hikari's, I would be like the handle to a sword. But at least all eyes would be on her, including mine, and not on me, I shrugged nonchalantly and made my way back to Hikari's room.

Hikari clapped ecstatically upon seeing me in the outfit. "I'm so glad it fits you! You look like a mushroom!"

I wondered how she managed to get my measurements right when I did not even recall discussing that with her.

"I have good eyes!" Hikari seemingly read my mind.

"Huh?"

She gestured to my outfit, "I guessed your measurements!" She declared proudly. "I've always loved Toad. I would like my date to be a cute and adorable mushroom!"

Though I felt the outfit was quite unflattering, as long as Hikari liked it, that is all that matters. My thought drifted to her condition, wondering if her cheerfulness was genuine or just a front she was putting up. I felt a pang of guilt for not doing more, but then I remembered that Hikari wanted me to treat her just as I normally would.

Unexpectedly, Hikari jumped towards me and gave me a tight hug. "Thank you, Arima!" I just stood there, not knowing what to do. It was extremely awkward for me, as I had never been hugged by a girl before, but I stood there in silence. We remained in that position for quite a while.

Hikari broke free after some time. Her face was slightly reddened. "Ahem! Don't read much into it! It is just a more westernised way of saying thanks!" Hikari explained hurriedly, her gaze shying away from mine.

After that, she quickly bid farewell to me – more like chased me out of her house – and I left for home.

CHAPTER 4:
THE DAY OF THE FESTIVAL

Two weeks had passed since the day I met Hikari at her place. The day of the Anime Festival had finally arrived. The Anime Festival was held on a Sunday at the Big Sight convention centre in Odaiba. It was an annual event where like-minded individuals met to embrace the anime culture. As Hikari and I lived in different districts in Tokyo, we decided to travel to the exhibition centre separately and meet there directly at 10am.

When I arrived at the exhibition centre, I was greeted with what you might expect, endless scores of attendees milling about. The entrance queue snaked beyond my vision. Some visitors were dressed in various anime characters. There were also people holding banners supporting their favourite anime characters, photographers, reporters etc. Looking at all the extravagant outfits around me, I broke into a cold sweat. The thought of me having to dress as a mushroom in front of thousands of people suddenly overcame me. I felt a pang of insecurity stab through my body as I realised my costume was rather simplistic when compared to the bold extravaganza around me.

With haste, I dropped Hikari a text: "Have you arrived? I'm queuing up to enter the exhibition hall."

Hikari responded: "So sorry! I thought we were meeting at 11am! I will be there in an hour! ;)"

I was frustrated. "You planned it, didn't you? You knew the queue would be long, so you scheduled the meeting an hour earlier to make me queue on your behalf!"

"Maybe? :P"

I let out an exasperated sigh and joined the queue.

One step after another, the seamlessly endless

queue became shorter and shorter. Soon, I neared the front of the queue. I glanced at the time and checked if Hikari had messaged me, but she hadn't.

Just as I was about to enter the exhibition hall, I heard someone call my name: "Arima! Arima! Wait for me!" I turned behind and saw Hikari running in my direction. She was panting profusely and said: "Thank god, I made it in time!" She hopped into the queue, ignoring annoyed sighs from behind us and we proceeded to enter the exhibition centre.

When we entered the exhibition hall, the place was packed. There were several booths, with some featuring live shows and special appearances by anime and manga creators, including voice actors. Additionally, there were booths filled with anime-related merchandise such as anime figurines and artwork by freelance illustrators. There were also stalls selling iconic anime food like melon pan, Takoyaki and Taiyaki.

With the huge variety of food to choose from, Hikari gleamed with excitement.

"I want to try everything here!" Hikari exclaimed. "Let's try the melon pan!" Hikari suggested while pulling me to the stall.

There was a long queue in front of the stall. "Arima, you queue for this while I'll queue for Takoyaki! Let's meet at the rest area after we are done buying the food!" Hikari instructed before darting off in the direction of the Takoyaki stall.

It took approximately fifteen minutes and I finally managed to grab my hands on two melon pans. The melon pans had a cookie-like crust with its signature pattern grid design. I quickly headed to the rest area to look for Hikari.

When I arrived at the rest area, I noticed Hikari was already there, munching away at the Takoyaki she bought.

"Here! Have some Takoyaki. It's delicious!" Hikari smiled and handed me a boat-like paper container in exchange for a melon pan.

There was only one Takoyaki ball left in the container.

"Seriously? You ate everything!" I complained.

"No! I specially reserved one for you!" Hikari expressed while having her mouth filled with melon pan.

"I guess I'm totally helpless towards her." I thought to myself as I picked the last Takoyaki ball and popped it into my mouth. The Takoyaki was soft on the outside and had a chewy texture on the inside. It was delicious, but it was a pity that I could only have one.

I went on to have the melon pan I bought. As I bit through the melon pan, the matcha ice cream filling inside oozed into my mouth. It was warm on the outside but cold on the inside. I savoured every bite.

After we were done eating, Hikari and I went to explore the other parts of the exhibition hall. As we walked around, we chanced upon an area filled with several people cosplaying as their favourite characters from various anime. Apparently, it was an area devoted to cosplaying where visitors were encouraged to showcase their cosplay outfits. There were also a few people cosplaying as Mario characters like Yoshi, Mario etc. But none as Toad. Hikari hastily said: "Quick! Go change into the outfit! I'll be changing into mine too! Let's meet here when we are done changing!"

After handing me my outfit, she zoomed off to the restroom to change into her outfit. I trudged to the restroom to change as well. It did not take long for me to change, but I was stalling for time in the restroom. I felt conflicted and tried to build the courage to step out of the restroom door.

After some deliberation, I decided to go back in the mushroom outfit. I averted my gaze and focused on the floor, but instead of shielding myself from attention, I attracted it.

When I was back at the location, Hikari was already there posing for photos with some attendees. The warmth in her eyes and the way she smiled at the attendees melted my heart. Her gentle persona highlighted a different side of her. My inner thoughts leaked: "Wow... She is gorgeous..."

While I was still captivated by her beauty, Hikari met my eyes and quickly walked over: "Hey! What took you so long? Come on! Let us pose for some photos!" She gently tugged my hand and pulled me towards a prominent spot.

There was already a crowd congregating there,

queuing to pose with and take photos of other cosplayers. Although the attention of the crowd was not on me, I felt as though I was being scrutinised due to me being self-conscious about what I was wearing. As soon as I noticed Hikari was posing for photos for one of the attendees, I seized the opportunity to escape. Out of nowhere, someone grabbed me by the head of the costume and pulled me downwards and I fell on my butt. I looked up and realised it was Hikari. Hikari had her arms crossed.

"Where do you think you are going?" Hikari asked assertively.

"What was that for?" I exclaimed.

Hikari extended her hand and offered to get me back up on my feet. I grabbed onto her hand and stood up.

Suddenly, several people started approaching us for pictures. Apparently, due to our commotion, the crowd felt that our actions were comical and portrayed the clumsiness of Toad and the assertiveness of Princess Peach, the characters we were cosplaying as.

Cameras started surrounding us, I was

extremely nervous and was sweating profusely. Noticing that I was feeling anxious, Hikari leaned closer to me and whispered: "Relax… Don't be so tense! Just follow my lead! I'm here for you!" I felt slightly more relaxed after hearing her words and slowly got accustomed to the cameras and my surroundings.

One photo was taken after another. In a blink of an eye, hours flew by. I turned to Hikari and noticed that her complexation did not look too good.

"Hey, Hikari! Let's take a break!" I suggested.

Hikari breathlessly replied: "Sure…! Let's take a break. I'm exhausted!"

I supported her to the rest area and reached out for a bottled water in my bag. "Here! Have some water, Hikari!" Hikari slowly sipped on the water. After drinking the water, she leaned her head on my shoulder and unknowingly fell asleep. Seeing her sleeping so soundly, I could not bear to wake her up. I grabbed my jacket from the bag and placed it over her gently.

Before I knew it, the anime festival was coming to an end. An announcement was made through the public address system: "Thank you for attending the Anime Festival! Visitors, please proceed to the exit! We hope to see you again next year!" Hikari slowly opened her eyes. I turned to Hikari and said: "You finally woke up!" She looked around her surroundings in confusion. Slowly, she realised she had been sleeping on my shoulder for hours. She became embarrassed, and her face turned red like a tomato.

Seeing how embarrassed Hikari was, I decided to tease her: "Hikari! I never knew you drool when you sleep!"

"No, I don't!" Hikari exclaimed.

I burst into laughter after seeing her flustered reaction. While we were still in the middle of an argument, a photographer walked towards us and passed me a couple of Polaroid photographs.

"Sorry for not asking permission. I could not help but take these photos of both of you!"

He then hurried off. We looked at the pictures and realised they were images of Hikari resting on my shoulder and her getting flustered while I was teasing her. Seeing those photographs, Hikari felt abashed and tried to grab them from me. Knowing that she was much shorter than me, I raised the photos up high till they were beyond her reach. She jumped with all her might to grab the photos back from me, nevertheless failed to reach them. Ultimately, she gave up after numerous attempts, and we exited the exhibition hall after changing out of our costumes.

While walking towards the train station, Hikari beamed with joy and said: "Thank you for today! And thank you for making my wish come true! My father used to bring me to these events before I was diagnosed with cancer. He would always wear the Toad outfit that you are wearing now. Seeing you in that consume really made me relive a childhood memory once again!" Hearing her say this, I felt bittersweet. Compared to the time we had our first conversation at the hospital, my concern towards Hikari started to grow.

However, knowing that her wish was to be herself and not be treated differently, I bottled up my feelings and nonchalantly replied: "I was forced to come here anyway!"

She chuckled and we left for home in our

separate ways after bidding each other goodbye.

While I was on the train on the commute back home, I took out the two photos I received from the photographer earlier during the event. I broke into a broad smile after looking at the first image of Hikari being flustered and blushing out of embarrassment. Then, I proceeded to look at the second image where Hikari was resting on my shoulder.

"She looks so vulnerable when she's asleep. A complete opposite to when she's awake." I thought to myself.

As I continued staring at the photo, I felt a tinge of sadness. The sight of Hikari sleeping peacefully, reminded me of her condition. And that she would be gone soon. I held my phone tightly in the other hand, resisting the urge to text Hikari, wondering how she was doing.

I realised my emotions were wavering. She had become more than an acquaintance to me now.

CHAPTER 5:
"ARE Y'ALL DATING?"

The next day I went to school as usual. Like any other day, I went to my usual corner at the cafeteria to have my lunch during recess. I had prepared a bento for lunch today. The bento consisted of cooked rice, with the mains of the bento being deep-fried tonkatsu, topped with a soft-serve pan omelette. The side dishes included a potato salad and two slices of watermelon.

"It's going to be a scrumptious lunch!" I said to myself. "Itadakimasu!" As I picked up my chopsticks and was about to dig in, Hikari appeared right in front of me. She proceeded to snatch the bento from me.

"Wow! The bento looks delicious! Itadakimasu!" She grabbed my chopsticks and started to eat my bento.

Seeing her munching my lunch away, I lashed out: "Hey! That's my lunch! Go get your own lunch!"

"Oishi! This omelette is so soft, so fluffy and oozy! It's so delicious!" Hikari exclaimed.

I yelled at her demanding that she return my bento at once, and she replied: "Okay! Fine! You can have some!" She picked a slice of tonkatsu using the chopsticks and attempted to feed it to me: "Say ahhh!" My cheeks and forehead were getting flushed.

"Knock it off Hikari!" I shouted.

"Oh! Arima, you look so nervous! You look so cute when you are flustered!" She teased.

Our interaction attracted the gaze of some of my classmates in the cafeteria. Suzuki Yue, Hikari's childhood friend, came over to our seat. "What are you doing, Hikari? Are y'all dating or what?" She questioned.

Hikari was flustered and stuttered: "N… No! We… We are definitely not dating!"

Yue responded: "Then why were you

attempting to feed him?”

Hikari nervously explained: “No, you must have seen wrongly! I was not attempting to feed Arima!” To ease the situation, Hikari quickly bid goodbye to me and grabbed onto Yue's arm hastily to pull her away.

Despite Hikari leaving, the stares of some students in the cafeteria did not ease. I could hear some whispers from some of my schoolmates.

“Why would Hikari date him?”

“What is the deal between them?”

“Who even is he?”

It felt extremely uncomfortable. I did my best to ignore the stares and murmurs and quickly gobbled my lunch before heading back to the classroom. “That was intense! Thank goodness it's over!” I thought to myself while walking back to the classroom.

Out of the blue, Yue appeared and grabbed me to a corner. She forcefully pushed me against the wall. I was horrified. “Hey… Yue! What's…up!” I stammered. Yue gave me a dead stare and slammed her fist against the wall. Yue grunted: “Hikari had so many suitors. All of which have better qualities than you. Even Hikari's ex-boyfriend, Minato (class monitor), is far better than you in terms of personality and appearance. Why did Hikari choose you out of all the other guys? You are undeserving of her!" With an intimidating tone, she threatened: "If I ever see you make Hikari cry, I swear you would wish you were never born!"

Hearing her words, I gulped a mouthful of saliva. My legs were starting to turn soft. Yue then proceeded to warn me to keep our interaction from Hikari and the consequence of not doing so before leaving. "What did Hikari tell Yue?" I mumbled to myself. I turned my head down to look at my watch only to realise that the lunch break was almost over. I took a moment to regain my composure and quickly went back to class, pretending that nothing had happened.

As I entered the classroom, rumours that Hikari and I were dating had already spread throughout the class. I averted the gaze of my classmates and quickly headed back to my seat.

The next few days of school were extremely

stressful and uncomfortable. I became the hot topic of the school. My classmates, who had no interest in talking to me, started asking me about my relationship with Hikari. I tried to deny having any romantic relationships with her, but no one was convinced. I felt it to be extremely draining to deal with the situation. To prevent attracting any more attention, I avoided Hikari as much as I could. Hikari continued to approach me in school, but I would make excuses to shun away from her. During my lunch breaks, I would head to the rooftop to have lunch where there was no one instead of the usual corner at the cafeteria.

Today, as usual, I proceeded to the rooftop to have lunch. "Finally! I can be alone!" I mumbled to myself as I pushed open the door leading to the rooftop.

To my surprise, Hikari was waiting by the rooftop door. She stared at me intensely. She angrily walked up towards me and yelled: "Why are you avoiding me?"

"I'm not avoiding you! I just want some time for myself," I said, defending my actions.

"Tsk!" She snapped, "I know why you are avoiding me! You're angry about the rumours in class, aren't you? But what's the big deal? Can't you just ignore them?"

Hearing her being so nonchalant about the situation she created, I erupted and shouted at her: "Are you even aware of the trouble you have caused me? You know how hard it is for me to put up with all your nonsense and tolerate your obnoxious behaviour!"

Tears started to flow down Hikari's cheeks, and Hikari ran down the stairs from the rooftop. Seeing her in tears was a sobering moment. Reflecting on my actions, I felt guilty for being too harsh towards her. I wanted to chase after her but stopped as I did not know how to comfort her. Since that incident, we had not spoken to each other.

Feeling a sense of guilt, I decided to pay Hikari a visit at her place over the weekend. As I arrived in front of her house gates, I started to have second thoughts. "Should I even pay her a visit? Would she even let me in? What if she doesn't take it too well?" Various concerns started to run through my mind. Unable to pluck up the courage, I ultimately decided to leave.

Just as I was about to do so, the gates opened. Hikari was standing across the other side of the gate. "Why are you walking in circles? If you are here to visit, just ring the doorbell." I took a few steps towards her and said: "Hikari, I'm sorry for saying those harsh words to…"

Before I could complete my sentence, Hikari ran towards me and hugged me tightly. In a quavering voice, Hikari expressed: "Baka! I should be the one to apologise. I was out of line! I failed to consider your feelings and position! Sorry, Arima!"

Instinctively, I wrapped my arms around her. "Hikari, I was also in the wrong. I shouldn't have shouted at you. I'm sorry." Hikari looked at me with a lighthearted smile and said: "I will be magnanimous and forgive you!" We then looked at each other and broke out laughing.

CHAPTER 6:
HOSPITALISED

About two weeks passed since that fateful day and Hikari was hospitalised. Due to the classes I had, I was only able to visit her during the weekends. Having been informed of the visitation hours by Hikari, I went to pay her a visit at the hospital. The weather that morning was rather chilly. I grabbed my sweater, which was hung on my bedroom door and made my way to the hospital.

Hikari was admitted to a private ward. When I arrived, there were no other visitors in her room. Hikari was dressed in a typical hospital gown. It was a short collarless gown tied from the back. She had a couple of tubes attached to her left wrist. She sat at the edge of her bed facing the window and was cheerfully humming to a tune while swinging her legs. When I called out to her, she let out a shriek and turned around. Noticing it was me, her face reddened, and she quickly burrowed her head under her blanket. I sat down on the chair beside her bed and patiently waited for her to break out from her blanket.

"Hey! Don't show up so abruptly! You gave me a scare! I could have died there!" Hikari exclaimed while still hiding under the blanket.

"Probably dying due to embarrassment?" I teased.

"Stop teasing me!" Hikari whined

"Fine. I'll stop teasing you. Stop hiding already!" I gently tapped her blanket, coaxing her to break out of her blanket.

Hikari slowly snuck her head out of her blanket and sat back up, pretending nothing had happened. She then proceeded to stretch out her right hand towards me.

"Huh? What do you want?" I looked at her cluelessly.

"Where is my visiting gift?" Hikari asked.

"What visiting gift?"

"You mean you came empty-handed?"

"What did you expect me to bring? I would not even come if you had not asked me to compile the materials for the classes you missed!"

"Humph!" Hikari pouted angrily, crossing her arms. "Go get me a gift now!" demanded Hikari.

"Sigh… What do you want me to get you?"

"Flowers! I love tulips!" cheered Hikari.

"Fine… I'll be back." I turned towards the door and was about to head out.

"Hehe… Arima, come back! I'm joking." Hikari giggled and stuck her tongue out. "But remember to bring me a gift next time, okay?" Hikari smiled widely.

"Sure… I'll remember to buy you one next time," I promised Hikari.

I went on enquiring about her condition.

"Don't worry! I'm fine. Some numbers were off when self-monitoring at home. I felt okay, but my parents insisted that I get it checked. Hence, I am being hospitalised and undergoing further observation. I'll probably be here for a week. After that, I'll be back in school!" Hikari explained.

"Hmm… By the time you are discharged, it would probably be a week before the beginning of the spring break," I responded.

"Oh yeah! We would have time to execute my second wish then!" She cheerfully replied.

"An entire week… Hmm…" A sudden doubt came to my mind. "Hey, Hikari! You would be away from school for a week, right? How did you break the news to your friends at school, especially Yue, without revealing your condition?" I questioned.

"I told them I had severe food poisoning. Everyone, especially Yue, seemed extremely worried about me, which makes it even harder for me to reveal my condition to them. What does the person who hugged me think about my story?" Hikari giggled.

"I guess I should respect the person who initiated the hug first!" I mocked initially. "But on a more serious note, I think you should tell Yue the truth. After all, she really cares about you!" I advised.

"Hmm… Your heart fluttered, didn't it? I was probably the first girl you ever hugged!" Hikari teased.

"Ah ahem! Let's start going through the content of the classes you have missed!" I leaned forward to reach out for the materials in my backpack.

"I haven't rested enough...!" whined Hikari.

"No, you already rested for a long time. Let's begin studying. Furthermore, you are the one who troubled me to compile everything taught during the classes you missed." I responded. I went on to pass her pages of summarised notes I made her for the classes she missed.

"Fine..." Hikari responded reluctantly.

I meticulously went through the content with her and tried my best to clarify any doubts she had regarding the lesson's content, probably rather unsuccessfully due to my inattentiveness in classes. For the most part though, Hikari was listening attentively.

After about two hours, we somehow manage to cover all the lesson content Hikari had missed. Despite my explanation being rather inadequate, Hikari complimented me for the effort and time I invested in going through the class content with her.

"Arima, thanks for spending time to go through the class material with me. I could understand most of it."

"You don't have to patronise me! I'm aware that my explanations were unclear!"

"Okay… It's true. But with some fine-tuning, I think you can even consider becoming a teacher in the future," Hikari suggested.

"That is not going to happen! It's obvious that I do not like to deal with humans!"

"If that was my dying wish? Would you do it in my stead?" Hikari asked.

I stared at her in disbelief.

"Just kidding! Don't look so tense!" She chuckled.

Looking at the clock, I realised it was about time for me to leave. "Anyways, I think I should go. Yue and the rest of your friends should be visiting you soon, right?"

"Arima, you can join us if you like! I'm sure the girls wouldn't mind having a handsome guy like you join in, would they?" Hikari responded sarcastically.

"Thanks, but no thanks!" I shrugged. "Take good care of yourself!" I said and headed for the door.

As I was about to exit the ward, the door suddenly banged open. "Hikari! Are you okay? How are you doing?" It was Yue. Upon seeing me in the ward, Yue glared at me as if she wanted to kill me.

"Tsk! You again? Why are you around Hikari all the time!" I could sense her frustration and the irritation she had towards me. I tried to avoid making eye contact with her as I felt it would be dangerous to look into the eyes of an aggressor. Hikari then leapt towards Yue and gave her a hug with one hand, seemingly to prevent any altercation between Yue and me.

"Yue! My stomach hurts so badly! Food poisoning is no fun!" She complained while waving goodbye to me with her other hand. Seizing the opportunity, I quickly left the room and headed back home.

Seeing how lively and vibrant she was, I felt relieved. The truth was that I feared that her condition had worsened, and she might die sooner than anticipated. Thankfully, she seemed fine. At least that was what I presumed.

CHAPTER 7:
SPRING VACATION

In a blink of an eye, it was the start of the spring vacation. Spring vacation usually lasts for about three weeks, from the third week of March to the second week of April. I drew the curtains apart in my room and stared blankly outside the window. It had been two weeks since Hikari was hospitalised – the duration of her hospitalisation was extended, although she had stated in previous text messages that she was doing fine. Frankly, when I was informed that Hikari would be staying there longer than anticipated, I was worried. I thought to myself: "I wonder how Hikari is doing?" Suddenly, my phone vibrated: "Beep!" It was a text from Hikari. The text read: "Why are you staring blankly outside your window? Are you thinking of me?" I panicked and immediately scanned the area outside the window; however, she was nowhere to be seen.

The next moment, the doorbell rang. I went to open to door.

It was Hikari. "Hi! Hi! I've been discharged from the hospital!" Hikari said in a cheerful voice. I was taken aback and had many questions run through my mind: "Why is she here? How does she know where I live?" But the first words I uttered when I saw her were: "Congrats on getting discharged. Glad that you are okay!"

Hikari nonchalantly replied: "Yah! Yah! Thanks for your concern!" Looking at how bubbly Hikari was, I felt a sense of relief. "So... Are we standing here for the rest of the day?" asked Hikari. Hikari's response snapped me back to reality: "Oh yeah! Come in!" I invited Hikari into my apartment.

"So, this is your place! It is quite modest!" Hikari commented and placed her handbag on the dining table. "Where is your room?" Hikari probed and began searching through the place. She proceeded to open one door after another. While she was about to open one of the doors, I panicked.

"Hey… Hey! What are you doing? Stop right there!"

"Eh? This surely must be your room! Is there something indecent in your room?" She said cheekily.

"That's not it!" I yelled.

Ignoring my warnings, she barged open the door. Hikari stood there in shock. I calmly walked towards her and spoke gently: "I told you not to open that door." I bowed slightly and performed two deeper bows before praying in silence. Seeing my actions, Hikari followed and did the same. After a few moments of silence, I gently closed the door, and we proceeded to the dining hall.

There was an awkward silence. After a while, Hikari spoke: "Sorry about that, Arima. I was not aware."

"No worries, it's fine!" To lighten the mood, I asked Hikari: "Have you had lunch yet? If not, I'll whip up a meal for us!"

"Sure… I've not had lunch." She responded.

I went on to prepare the ingredients required

and started cooking.

"By the way… The pictures hung on the altars. Who are they?" Hikari asked hesitantly.

I answered: "They are my parents." Seeing that it piqued her interest, I continued explaining: "They were involved in a car accident and passed away about a few years back, just before I entered high school. I've lived here on my own ever since!"

Out of concern, Hikari enquired: "How have you been supporting yourself all this while? How did you even manage till now?"

I further elaborated: "My Uncle sends me a monthly allowance every month, so I don't really have to worry about my finances. The only downside I see would be having to do all the household chores myself. But I am already used to doing them! So, it's fine!" I responded with a lighthearted tone. Unexpectedly, Hikari hugged me from behind.

"Hey! Get off me! It's dangerous! I'm in the middle of cooking!" I exclaimed.

Hikari spoke in a gentle but emotional voice: "All these years… I cannot imagine nor comprehend what you must have endured. But despite all that…you have turned out alright. If your parents were still around, I think they would have been proud of you Arima!" Hearing Hikari's words, I felt a tug in my heart. All this while, I had buried my emotions and kept telling myself everything will be alright. Days and unknowingly years have gone by, and I thought the death of my parents was something I had come to accept. However, hearing Hikari's words, a wave of emotions washed over me. Tears flowed down my cheeks uncontrollably. Those were the words I have always yearned to hear, that my parents would be proud of who I turned out to be.

"Hiss! Hiss!" A whistling sound was emitting from the pot, and the soup I brewed was starting to overflow. Hearing the whistling sound, I snapped back to reality. Immediately, I wiped the tears off my face and gently broke free from Hikari's hug to turn off the stove. "Hikari, can you please wait at the dining hall? It's a little challenging to cook with you around, restricting my movements." I spoke softly.

"Sorry about that, Arima! I'll wait outside!" Hikari responded before proceeding to the dining area. I then continued to finish cooking the meal.

After another twenty minutes, I finished cooking the meal and served it to Hikari and myself. "I prepared omelette fried rice and miso soup! Hope you like my cooking!" I spoke. While eating the meal, Hikari was awfully quiet. "Does it taste that bad?" I asked.

"No, it tastes really good!" Hikari commented. If the food was not the problem, I figured it was due to the earlier incident.

In an attempt to stimulate a conversation, I enquired: "By the way, why did you come here today? Wasn't it to discuss your second wish?"

Feeling uncertain, Hikari replied: "Yes, it was but…" Seeing her looking downcast, I attempted to provoke her: "Stop trying to beat around the bush! You are always straightforward and demanding. Where did all that spirit and energy go? I've already promised to carry out the three wishes on your bucket list, and I intend to fulfil them, so you need not feel apologetic!"

"Hey! That's rude! I am not demanding!" She complained. "Okay then, back to the topic, my second wish is for you to explore Kyoto with me. I would like to view the sunset at the summit of Fushimi Inari Taisha!" She responded with a smile.

"I doubt your parents would even agree to it!" I remarked.

"I have my ways. You do not have to worry about that!" She replied while reaching for a notebook in her bag. "Ta-da! I planned the entire literary already and even booked the Shinkansen tickets. We will depart in the morning the day after! You cannot break your promise, okay?" She responded cheerfully.

"Fine! Thanks for being so considerate as always!" I said sarcastically.

"Thanks for the compliment!" She replied with a smile.

"It wasn't a compliment!" I snared. But I was glad she went back to how she usually was. After finishing the lunch, I prepared, we bid our goodbyes, and Hikari left for home.

CHAPTER 8:
THE SECOND WISH

The following day I headed to Tokyo station, the station we were departing from, early in the morning. I carried a backpack which contained my essentials and toiletries. The weather that day was clear and cloudy. When I arrived, Hikari was already there. She was dressed casually, in a sky-blue sleeveless dress and was wearing heels. Beside her was a four-wheeled beige luggage bag which was almost twice her size.

I looked at Hikari in dismay. "What's in that gigantic luggage of yours? A dead body?" I teased.

Feeling offended by my comment, Hikari replied: "Hey! I only packed my essentials, okay?"

"Your essentials? Your luggage is almost five times the size of my backpack?"

"Humph! Girls have more essentials than guys. Stop judging me!" Hikari placed her hands on her hips and said angrily.

"Okay! Enjoy carrying that heavy luggage of yours!" I mocked.

"It's fine since you are carrying it!" Hikari smiled at me cheekily and shoved her luggage to me before skipping her way towards the train station.

"Hey! Your luggage!" I yelled.

Hikari turned towards me and bowed slightly. She then proceeded to shout across: "Thanks for carrying my luggage for me!" before running into the train station.

I was left to carry her luggage. I painfully lugged both of our luggages and entered the train station to look for Hikari.

Hikari was standing in front of a bento stall. I walked up to Hikari and asked: "Which platform are we supposed to head to?" but she took no notice of me and was entirely fixated on the menu.

I tried calling out to her again: "Hikari? Which

platform are we supposed to head to?" but she continued to ignore me.

"Which bento should I get? There are so many choices to choose from," Hikari mumbled to herself while smacking her lips.

"Hikari!" I shouted.

Hikari jumped in shock. "Hey, you do not need to scream, I'm right beside you!"

"If you had given me a reply, I wouldn't have resorted to shouting," I explained.

"Okay… Anyways, let's grab something to eat on the train," Hikari suggested and continued to stare at the wide selection of bento available.

"Sure! But what time is the train departing?" I enquired.

Hikari took out our Shinkansen tickets from her pocket and chucked them at me. "Here, help check it!"

Our departure time was 8.50am. We still had approximately twenty minutes left. Noticing that there was limited time, I swiftly placed an order for the tonkatsu bento, which supposedly was their best seller, avoiding the hassle to go through the entire menu.

"Have you decided on your order?" I asked Hikari.

"There are so many to choose from! It's so hard to decide." Hikari complained.

"Our train is leaving soon. You need to decide quickly!" I chased.

"I know! But I just can't decide!" Hikari whined.

"Hey! Can you please hurry? At this rate, we'll miss the train!" I spoke in agitation.

Hikari remained indecisive. In the end, Hikari did not order a bento and boarded the train empty-handed.

Within minutes, the Shinkansen departed. Not long after we departed from the station, I heard a rumbling noise coming from Hikari. I looked to Hikari and noticed her face was blushing.

"It's not me!" Hikari denied it anxiously.

"She must be hungry. I really wanted to try the bento, but I guess she can have mine," I thought to myself. "Here, you can have it!" I nonchalantly passed the bento I bought to Hikari.

Hikari beamed with joy as she saw the bento and started to gobble down the food. "Slow down! Nobody is going to snatch it from you!" I said.

After a while, Hikari tapped on my shoulder. I turned to her to see her handing me a half-finished bento.

"Here! You can have half of it! Thanks for sharing your bento with me," thanked Hikari.

I was a little surprised. "Didn't think she would even consider sharing," I thought to myself.

"Hey! Take it already! Why do you look so shocked?" She questioned. Still in disbelief, I took the bento from her and proceeded to eat it. The bento was delicious. The juice oozed out of tonkatsu with every bite I took.

As I was enjoying the bento, Hikari smirked and cheekily said: "I just kissed you, Arima! You used the same utensils as mine! Did you enjoy it?" Hearing her remark, I almost choked on the food.

"Are you that childish, Hikari?" I snarled. Seeing my reaction, Hikari held her stomach and burst out laughing. To be honest, I did not even notice that till she mentioned it.

As the train ride continued, a doubt came to mind. "By the way, are your parents really okay with you going on this trip?" I probed.

"With only a few months left to live, my parents would probably accede to any of my requests. But knowing how overprotective they are towards me, they probably would not agree to let me travel out of Tokyo with a friend, let alone someone of the opposite sex. So, I lied that I was having a sleepover at Yue's house! I told Yue to cover for me," Hikari said, trying to justify her actions.

I exclaimed: "That's horrible! You…"

Before I could finish my sentence, Hikari screamed in excitement and pointed towards the window: "Look, Arima! Cherry blossoms!" Hikari's scream was gathering a bit of attention from the train. Noticing the stares, I told Hikari to lower her volume. In a cheerful tone, Hikari asked: "Aren't the cherry blossoms so beautiful, they are so small and delicate!"

"Yes, they are!" I replied while admiring the beauty of the cherry blossoms. Collectively they looked like a soft cloud with a tinge of pink. When the wind blew, the petals danced freely with the breeze, like snowflakes from the first snow.

After a while, Hikari's expression turned cold, and she mumbled a few words. I could not comprehend what Hikari was saying as she was too soft. "What did you say, Hikari?" I asked.

Hikari quickly changed her expression and replied with a warm smile: "Nothing, just admiring the beauty of the cherry blossoms!" I knew something was bothering her, but I decided not to probe further, knowing that it was something she did not want me to know.

Not long after, an announcement was made through the intercom: "We'll soon be arriving at Kyoto. Thank you for riding the Shinkansen again today. After departing Kyoto, the next stop is Nagoya." We finally arrived at our destination, Kyoto station.

"Yay! We finally arrived!" Hikari cheered. "Is that the smell of ramen, Arima?" Hikari asked.

I scoffed at Hikari's remark and said: "Is food all that you think about? How can there be ramen here?"

Hikari pouted her lips and stared at me

angrily. We then proceeded to take the escalator, which led us to the ticket gates. The instant I exited the ticket gates, I was hit with an unexpected sensation that made me doubt my perceptions. I could smell ramen, just as she had mentioned before.

There was indeed a ramen stall located just outside the ticket gates. Noticing the ramen stall, Hikari smirked and mocked: "I guess your sense of smell is the problem, not mine! Hehe!"

Although I would hate to admit it, Hikari was right this time. "Fine. You were right!" I acknowledged my mistake.

"Since you were at fault, you'll treat me to ramen!" Hikari ordered. I gave in to her request, and we had ramen for lunch. Apparently, Kyoto-style ramen is one of the must-try delicacies in Kyoto. The ramen was delicious. The ramen had an opaque, gravy-like chicken broth loaded with egg noodles and four slices of cha shu topped with green onions. We were allowed to decide on the level of firmness of our noodles. Apparently, there are a total of six levels to choose from "Bari-Yawa" (extra soft) to "Harigane" (extra-extra firm). To be honest, I had no knowledge of this. To prevent embarrassing myself, whatever Hikari ordered, I just followed suit. Thankfully, it turned out alright.

After lunch, Hikari suggested we start heading to Fushimi Inari Taisha, a shrine dedicated to the Kami Inari, a Shinto god. Apparently, it was also a well-known attraction in Kyoto. I had no objections. After all, it was her wish to visit the shrine. Furthermore, I had never been to Kyoto and was unaware of the locations we should visit.

The distance from Kyoto station to our destination was a fifteen-minute commute via the local train. Thus, we boarded the local train and headed to the shrine. I was expecting the train to be packed like in Tokyo. However, the trains were surprisingly less crowded, and we even managed to get seats for the both of us. But ultimately, I was the only one seated.

Throughout the train ride, Hikari was constantly moving about, peering through the train windows to observe the scenery like a little kid. Her actions made me wonder if she was really dying soon.

CHAPTER 9:
FUSHIMI INARI TAISHA

Soon after, we arrived at Inari station, the station which was the station closest to Fushimi Inari Taisha. Hikari decided to leave her luggage at a coin locker in the station and transferred most of her essential items to my bag.

When we first exited from Inari station, we could see the first torii gate of the shrine. The distance between the station and the main entrance of Fushimi Inari Taisha was about a five-minute walk. Unsure of the path to reach our destination, we decided to follow the crowd. Rows of shops were lined up along the route we took. The shops had a traditional appearance similar to that of old Japanese houses. Some shops sold snacks like fortune cookies and inari-shaped rice crackers, while others sold inari-themed pottery and tableware. There were also shops providing yukata rentals services. "Let's try on a yukata!" Hikari suggested while pointing at a shop renting yukata. Hikari then pulled me by my sleeve and dragged me to the shop against my will. A large poster hanging in front of the shop "Day rental ~ ¥3,200 accessories included!"

As we stepped into the stall, we were greeted by a wide selection of yukatas, from bright coloured flora patterns to more subtle and modern geometric designs. There were so many choices to choose from in the shop. Looking at the wide variety of yukatas, Hikari could not hold her excitement and quickly started browsing through the yukatas. I was not keen on wearing a yukata, so I just sat in a corner waiting for her.

"Arima, do you think this light pink yukata with white lily flowers or the one in white with blue and pink morning glory will look better on me?" asked Hikari.

"I think the one in pink will look better," I

commented.

"Okay, I'll go with the pink one then!" Hikari replied with a satisfied smile.

Hikari proposed that I should try on a yukata too, but I was not keen on wearing one. She began to whine and coax me to wear a yukata with her. This caught the store owner's attention, and she even sided with Hikari to persuade me to put on a yukata. I felt pressured and eventually gave in to prevent any further embarrassment. I did not know which yukata to choose and had the stall owner decide for me. The stall owner picked a grey yukata with a striped design, stating that it would match the yukata chosen by Hikari. We were also given a pair of geta (wooden sandals) and an obi (a sash) matching the yukata of our choice. For the ladies, a kinchaku, also known as a traditional carry bag, and a hair arrangement service were also provided. As the procedure for males was relatively shorter, I finished changing into the yukata outfit before Hikari was done and was waiting patiently for her. Though the wait was a mere twenty minutes, it felt like an eternity.

Finally, Hikari was done changing. As she

walked towards me in her yukata, my jaw dropped. I had never seen this side of Hikari. The yukata was not extravagant looking, but it brought out every inch of Hikari's charm to the greatest extent. She looked so feminine and flattering in the yukata. I caught myself staring too much and immediately averted making eye contact with Hikari.

"You look good in the yukata!" complimented Hikari.

"Y… You too!" I stammered.

Looking at how beautiful she was in the outfit, it made it difficult to look at her.

"You two look great in the yukatas! Like the perfect couple!" The store owner commented.

Hearing that Hikari and I were treated as a couple, I was flustered, and my face reddened. My palms felt sweaty. I took a quick glance at Hikari. To prevent Hikari from feeling uncomfortable, I frantically explained to the store owner that we were not a couple.

The store owner gave me a wink. She then leaned forward and whispered softly to me: "She's an eye candy, isn't she? Make her yours if you can!" The store owner's comment made me abashed.

"What did the store owner say to you? Why is your face so red?" Hikari asked.

"Nothing! It's just the weather!" I explained. Upon saying that, I realised how stupid I was. We were in an air-conditioned room all this while. Surprisingly, Hikari did not probe further. We then exited the shop and headed to the entrance of the shrine.

Along the way to the shrine, I was perplexed by Hikari's reaction back at the shop when the shop owner misunderstood that we were a couple. I recalled she was smiling when I took a quick glance at Hikari. Were my eyes playing tricks on me? Now that I thought about it, Hikari didn't even try to clear the misunderstanding. Does she not mind when others assume we are a couple? I must be overthinking, she probably found it too troublesome to correct a stranger. I must've been mistaken. It was probably just my imagination, I convinced myself.

Not long after, we arrived at the entrance of the shrine. What stood before us was a gigantic torii gate. Behind it was the majestic two-storied romon gate. It had two fox statues guarding it. According to the Shinto religion, foxes are thought to be messengers of Kami Inari.

Hikari reached out for a notebook in my bag. It was the notebook she had prepared for this trip. Hikari flipped to a section titled Fushimi Inari Taisha, which contains various information about the shrine and even steps to follow. I was dumbfounded. "My god! I can't believe she actually did this!" I thought to myself.

Hikari started playing the role of our tour guide, explaining to me the history of the shrine. "Hmm… According to my research, this two-story romon gate was donated in 1589 by the famous regent Toyotomi Hideyoshi. Behind it should be the main hall, also known as honden, where believers pay their respect to Kami Inari. But first, it is customary for us to purify ourselves at the water basin (tsukubai) before entering. There are a total of seven steps. First, bow slightly towards the water basin. Then holding the dipper with your right hand, scoop some water and pour it into your left hand. Next, switch hands and…"

I interrupted Hikari: "I'll pass on this. It's too troublesome. I don't even believe in Shintoism anyway!" Hikari was annoyed by my statement and insisted I show respect to the culture. It was the first time I had seen Hikari mad. Seeing her persistence, I obliged.

"Fine! I will follow the steps accordingly!"

After purifying ourselves, we passed the romon gate, which led us to the honden. The honden had a majestic appearance. It was covered with ornamental carvings, and the exterior was painted with vivid colours. There were fences surrounding the honden, and visitors were only allowed to pray from outside the honden and were not permitted to enter the premises of the building.

"Let's pay respects and convey our wishes to Kami Inari!" Hikari said while eagerly dragging me towards the queue forming in front of the honden. "Here's a coin for you!" Hikari reached for her purse and passed me a 100-yen coin for the offering while taking one for herself. When it was our turn to pray, Hikari rang the bell gently and placed the offering into a box. Then she bowed twice and clapped twice before covering her eyes and praying fervently in silence. After observing Hikari's actions, I mimicked her actions in their entirety.

"What should I pray for?" I thought to myself. The only thing I wanted was for Hikari and me to remain the way we are now, but I knew I was asking for the impossible.

Wishes that were harder to come through were more likely to be prayed for. I prayed sincerely that Hikari's condition would improve, and we can continue spending time like this. After conveying our prayers, we bowed our heads once more and left.

Despite being curious about what Hikari wished for, I did not feel the need to ask as prayers were something personal.

"Arima, what did you pray for?" Hikari enquired.

"I don't see the need to share my prayer requests with you."

"Did you wish for something inappropriate?" Hikari asked with a smirk on her face.

"Seriously? That's what she thinks of me!" I muttered under my breath.

"Or... Don't tell me you wished for something bad to happen to me so that I will die sooner! You're the worst!" accused Hikari.

"Why would I wish for that?" I defended myself against her accusation.

Hikari laughed hysterically and mocked: "Arima! You look so hilarious when you are anxious!"

I could not help but turn a deaf ear to her remarks.

"Speaking of which, can you wait here for a while? I need to use the washroom." Hikari asked.

"Ok. I'll wait here," I replied.

Hikari then zoomed off in a direction. "Isn't the washroom direction right in front?" I thought to myself. I called out to Hikari to signal to her that the closest washroom was in the opposite direction to the one she was heading, but she did not seem to hear me. The weather was scorching hot, and I could feel the heat penetrating through my skin. To avoid being cooked under the sun, I sought shelter under a tree while waiting patiently for Hikari.

Suddenly, a gust of wind blew towards me, and a mysterious childlike voice emitted from the winds: "Hehe… We'll soon meet each other!"

Upon hearing the voice, I looked to my surroundings, but no one was there. I was bewildered and wondered: "Who was that and where did the voice come from?"

"Hey, Arima! I'm back!" Hikari shouted while running towards me.

I looked at my watch and realised that it had been thirty minutes. "Took you long enough!" I said in an annoyed tone.

"Hey! Be more understanding! Girls take longer, okay!" Hikari yelped.

"Fine… Let's start hiking." I suggested.

We then walked towards the start of the hiking trail, located behind the honden.

CHAPTER 10:
THE HIKE

Soon we arrived at the entrance to the hiking trail. I looked up the hiking trail in awe. In front of us was a route covered with a seemingly endless stretch of torii gates. Every gate was donated by individuals or corporations, where the size of the gate reflected the donation amount. The larger the gate, the bigger the donation amount was. The poles of every gate had the engravings of the donor and the date of the donation. Even the smaller gates had a minimum donation of 400,000 yen. "Wow, the money donated to build this shrine is immense!" I thought to myself.

While I was buried in my thoughts, Hikari shouted: "Arima! Look here!" Hearing Hikari's voice,

I instinctively turned to her.

"Ka-chick!" Hikari snapped a picture of me using her mobile phone. Looking at the picture, Hikari burst out laughing.

"Delete that!" I yelled.

"No way! It's payback for the time in the anime convention!" Hikari responded cheekily. She continued to make fun of how ridiculous I looked in the picture.

While Hikari was distracted, I quickly whipped out my phone and took a close-up shot of Hikari.

"Stop it! Delete that!" Hikari demanded.

I jolted a few meters ahead of Hikari and taunted: "I'm not deleting it! Catch me if you can! See you at the top!" I then waved goodbye to Hikari and continued running up the trail.

"Stop right there! I am coming for you!" Hikari started chasing after me while I tried getting as far away from her as I could.

"Ah!" I heard a loud shriek from behind. I was stunned by the sound and instinctively turned behind. Hikari was laying face down on the ground.

Due to her usual pranks, I assumed she was pretending. "Hikari, I know you are faking it! I'm not falling for it!" I shouted. Hikari laid there motionlessly. "Stop playing!" I yelled but she continued laying there motionlessly. Fear started to creep in. "H… Hey Hikari are you o…okay?" I stammered. There was still no response from Hikari. I immediately ran towards Hikari and gently shook her, but she stayed completely silent. I started to panic. The thought that she might have died overwhelmed me. I yelled: "Hikari! Hikari! Wake up! Can you hear me?"

Suddenly, I heard a chuckle. "Hehe! It's so funny! Your reaction was priceless," laughed Hikari. Seeing that Hikari was fine, I heaved a sigh of relief, but that relief slowly turned into agitation.

In a stern voice, I warned: "Don't ever play me like that again!"

Hikari replied with slight remorse: "Ok… I'm sorry." She proceeded to tease: "But it was extremely funny hearing how nervous you were when you thought I was dead!"

"It is not funny!" I replied in a serious tone.

"Anyways… Delete that picture as you promised!" Hikari ordered.

"No! I refuse. That does not count!"

Hikari then locked her arms with mine, reluctant to let me go till I deleted that photo.

"Get off me!"

"Not until you delete it!"

"Fine, fine! Let go of me!"

I went to my phone's gallery to locate the image and clicked on the delete button in front of Hikari. Seeing that the embarrassing picture of her was deleted, Hikari smiled widely and released her grip on me. We then continued our hike.

After about thirty minutes, Hikari started gasping for air and was panting heavily. Observing how exhausted she was, I suggested that we took a break. Hikari reached for a bottled water in her kinchaku, only to find an almost empty bottle. Hikari shook the nearly empty bottle vigorously, attempting to salvage every last drop of water in the bottle. Having insufficient water, Hikari turned to me and asked if I had any water to spare, but I too ran out of water.

"According to what I read up previously, there should be a rest stop located somewhere in the middle of the trail, where we can get water. Let's proceed to the rest stop," suggested Hikari.

Looking at how exhausted Hikari was, I volunteered to get water on our behalf. I instructed Hikari to stay where she was while I searched for the rest stop.

Ten minutes had passed. I muttered to myself: "Where exactly is the rest stop?" Suddenly, I encountered an intersection. In front of me were two separate paths. "Crap! Which of these paths leads to the rest stop?" I thought to myself. I tried to search for directions using my phone, but there was no internet connection. There wasn't anybody around that I could seek help from either. As I was still deliberating on which path to take, an old lady shortly appeared and was walking towards the route on the right. She was hunched back and held a wooden walking stick. The walking stick had engraving, which seemed to resemble foxes. I quickly approached the old lady to seek directions.

"Sorry to bother you. May I enquire which of

these paths leads to the rest stop?"

Speaking in a slow manner, the old lady replied: "The path on the right leads to the rest stop, but it would take another twenty minutes to reach there."

"Another twenty minutes! That will be too long!" I thought to myself, constantly worried about Hikari's condition. "Sorry, is there a shorter alternative where I can get water?" I asked and explained my situation to the old lady.

The old lady pointed to the path on the left and said: "If I recall correctly, there is an old shrine nearby. There should be a water basin there where you can fill your bottle."

I was relieved to hear that there was a closer water point. I turned to the old lady to thank her, but she vanished. "This is weird? She was here just a moment ago." Despite being bewildered by the situation, getting water for Hikari took priority. With haste, I quickly pace towards the left path in search of the old shrine.

Compared to the path I had taken so far; this path was uneven and covered with fallen leaves and tree branches. As I walked deeper into the route, the torii gates that covered the entire trail of the hike so far gradually disappeared. Seeing the unfamiliar terrain, I questioned myself: "Is this the correct path, or did that old lady direct me wrongly? Should I head back?"

CHAPTER 11:
THE ENCOUNTER

"Plop! Plop! Plop!"

"What is that sound?" I wondered.

I decided to follow the direction of the sound. The sound was getting louder and louder, and I figured that I must be getting closer to the source. Suddenly, I hit a roadblock. A huge boulder stood before me. I leaned towards the boulder.

"The sound… It's behind this rock!"

I tried to push the boulder aside with every ounce of my strength, but the boulder would not even budge.

"I guess I've no choice but to turn back. What a waste of time!" I grumbled.

As I was about to make my way back to the intersection, I heard a rustling noise coming from the bushes. Out of curiosity, I went to the bushes to take a look. To my surprise, there was a fox. The fox had fur as white as snow and its eyes appeared to be sparkling. I rubbed my eyes with my fingers to ensure that it was not my imagination. It was unusual to see foxes, let alone a white one. I carefully took out my phone in hopes of taking an image of the white fox without scaring it away. Just as I was about to snap a photo, the white fox suddenly leapt off. Instinctively, I proceeded to chase after it. I cut through several bushes, trying to catch up with the white fox. But ultimately, it burrowed in a hole under a tree which was beyond my reach. "What a waste!" I grunted.

After regaining my composure, I looked around and was unaware of where I was. "Wait, where exactly am I?" I questioned myself. I was so caught up with the white fox that I lost my way. A bright light suddenly radiated from behind the tree. The light was so bright that it blinded my eyes. I used my hand to shield my eyes from its glare and slowly walked towards it. The light slowly dimmed as I approached, and a rundown shrine appeared before my eyes. The building, which appeared to be the honden, seemed to be unkept for years and was covered with overgrown vines. There were also lanterns hung around the entrance of the honden.

"This must be the shrine the old lady was talking about," I mumbled to myself. I entered the shrine with caution and scanned through the surroundings. There was a water basin beside the honden, which had water flowing from a pipe leading from the top of the mountain. Behind the water basin was a path which was apparently blocked by a boulder which was similar to the one I saw previously. I walked towards the water basin and looked down. The water in the water basin was surprising crystal clear. I scoped a mouthful of water with my hands and drank it. "The water is really fresh!" I thought to myself and continued to down more water. When I was done hydrating myself, I reached out for the bottle in my bag and filled it up with the water in the basin.

After filling up the bottle, I looked at my watch and learned that it had been close to thirty minutes since I left Hikari. Realising that I had been gone for too long, I quickly headed for the exit of the shrine. As I approached the exit, a voice emitted through the air: "Arima, you are finally here!"

"Who's there? Show yourself!" I shouted.

"Wait this voice… It sounds familiar." I racked my brains trying to recall where I heard this voice. It soon became clear to me. The voice was the same childlike voice I heard while waiting for Hikari to return from the washroom. A gust of wind blew and the white fox I had seen previously appeared before me in front of the honden entrance of the old shrine. The white fox spoke: "We meet at last, Arima!"

"W… Who are you? H… How do you know my name?" I stammered in fear upon seeing the talking fox.

"I have observed your life on the sidelines, and I am intrigued by you. Soon, we'll meet again, and when that time comes, I'd love to see the decision you will make."

"What do you mean? Explain yourself!" I called out to the white fox. My vision started to get blurry, and before I knew it, I fell to the ground unconscious.

"Wake up! Arima! Wake up!" I heard a voice. I also felt some water dripping on my face. I slowly opened my eyes, and I saw someone who seemed to look like Hikari in front of me. "Wait, it is Hikari!" The person who I thought resembled Hikari was indeed Hikari. I looked around my surroundings and noticed that I was laying on Hikari's knee. Feeling embarrassed, I quickly sat up and immediately apologised to Hikari for my actions. "Arima, what happened? Are you okay?" Hikari asked in a quavering voice while grabbing onto my arm tightly.

I was utterly confused: "Why am I here? I was at the old shrine a moment ago. The last thing I remembered was me falling to the ground."

I went on to ask Hikari why she was here and how she found me. She explained the entire situation to me. Apparently, Hikari left to look for me after waiting for an hour and found me laying unconscious. Hikari looked at me with tears welling in her eyes.

"Please don't scare me like that! I thought something bad had happened to you! I kept calling out to you, but you remained unconscious."

I apologised to Hikari for the panic I had caused and assured her that I was alright.

After Hikari was more composed, I enquired: "Hikari, wasn't there two paths to take? How did you know which path to take?"

"There is only one path up here. What are you talking about?"

I was certain that there was an intersection with two paths, but Hikari insisted that there was only one way up here. Seeing my persistence, Hikari suggested that we hike down the trail to the spot where she was asked to wait for me.

We proceeded our way down the trail, and soon we arrived at the place where Hikari was told to wait for me. "This was where I waited for you!" Hikari said while pointing towards the side. It was indeed the location. The torii gate located beside the spot had a red cross engraved on the bottom of one of its poles which matched my recollection. There was indeed only one path, and the intersection was nowhere to be seen. I was in an utter state of confusion.

"Huff! Huff!" Hikari panted heavily. I turned to Hikari and saw a worn-out look on her face. The walking must have drained her. I instantaneously recalled that Hikari needed water. That totally slipped my mind.

I quickly pulled myself back together. I reached out for the bottle in my bag and passed it to Hikari. "Here! Have some water!" Hikari took the bottle from my hands and gulped down more than half of the water in the bottle within an instant.

"Wait! The water… I got it from the water basin at the old shrine! The intersection was surely there!" I thought to myself.

Recalling the unsettled look on Hikari's face, I decided to not probe further and kept my thoughts to myself to prevent Hikari from worrying.

"Arima, are you really okay?" Hikari asked.

"Yeah! I'm fine," I replied.

It was obvious that the Hikari was still disturbed by what had happened.

"Anyways, let's continue hiking. We want to reach the peak before sunset, right?" I said, trying to divert Hikari's attention.

I stood up and dusted my pants before reaching my hand out to Hikari: "Come on! Let's go!" Hikari looked at me with uncertainty, but she eventually grabbed my hand to support herself up, and we continued our hike.

CHAPTER 12:
THE CONFESSION

We passed the rest stop, and soon we covered about three-quarters of the hiking trail. Hikari's pace gradually became slower, and she began to lag behind me. I turned to Hikari and asked how she was feeling. "I'm tired! My feet are hurting!" Hikari complained. Hikari then squatted down and hugged her knees tightly, curling up like a ball.

"What time is it?" Hikari enquired.

"It's almost 5pm," I replied.

Hearing that it was close to 5pm, Hikari supported herself up and tried to continue the hike, but she appeared to be in tremendous pain with every step she took.

"Hikari, there's still time. Let's take a short break." I proposed.

"No… We'll miss the sunset at this rate!" Hikari replied breathlessly.

After much persuasion, Hikari gave in and agreed to rest for a while. I sat Hikari down and attempted to remove her sandals.

"What are you doing? It's dirty!" Hikari exclaimed.

"It's fine!" I assured.

I gently took off her sandals. Hikari's feet were covered with blisters and were swelling due to excessive walking. Seeing the condition of Hikari's feet, I suggested that we stop and return to the entrance as she could get hurt if she continued hiking.

"Arima, I want to see the sunset! I will continue hiking," Hikari insisted.

"Even if we continue the hike! At the current pace you are walking, there is no way we'll reach in time. Let's call it a day and head back!" I reasoned.

Upon hearing my words, Hikari was downcast but slowly became cheerful again.

"Arima! I've an idea! We can make it if you

piggyback me up the summit," suggested Hikari.

"No! That is out of the question!" I replied without hesitation as I knew piggybacking her to the summit would probably be a task too immense for me.

"Pleeeease!" Hikari looked at me with wistful eyes.

"Stop acting like a kid! Acting cute will not change my mind! Moreover, it would be extremely straining to carry you to the summit." I explained and proceeded to turn away from her.

In a disappointed tone, Hikari said: "Okay... I'll rest for a bit, and we'll head back down."

I took a glance at Hikari. Her eyelids drooped, and her eyes were looking down. The ends of her lips pulled downwards. She looked dejected and depressed. Guilt and sympathy started to creep into me. "This may well be one of her last wishes. Will I regret my decision in the future when she is no longer around?" I pondered.

I looked at my watch and noticed that it was just past 5pm. "We still have about thirty minutes. We can still make it if we go now!" I said to myself. After changing out of the rental sandals to my original shoes which were kept in my bag, I went in front of Hikari. I turned my back towards her and bent my knees slightly while wearing my bag in front.

"Eh!" Hikari was bewildered.

"Hop on! Before I change my mind," I said in an indifferent tone.

Hikari gently placed her arms around my shoulders. I pulled my arms beneath Hikari's legs to join my hands and straighten my knees. "Grab on tight!" I instructed Hikari and continued hiking the mountain.

Sweat started pouring down my face, and my breathing became heavier as the hike continued. Hikari slipped off my back a few times, but I managed to secure her in time to prevent her from falling. "Are you okay, Arima? If it is too much, we should just head back?" Hikari asked out of concern. My legs were sore, and the cumulative weight of Hikari and I was increasingly unbearable. But I was determined to reach the summit no matter what it takes. "Don't worry! I can handle it! Just take a break and we'll be there in no time!" I assured Hikari. I gritted my teeth tightly and shook off any thoughts of tiredness. I kept pushing myself with each step. It was a long-enduring hike, but finally, I could catch a glimpse of what appeared to be the summit. In a soft and breathy voice, I spoke: "We made it in time! There are still five minutes before the sunset!" I gently lowered Hikari down. The moment she was on the ground, I immediately sat down to catch my breath. I was dead beat.

"Here. Wipe your sweat with this!" Hikari handed me a handkerchief.

I looked at Hikari and asked: "Are you sure?"

Hikari smiled, "Take it! I insist!"

"Thanks!" I took the handkerchief and wiped the sweat off my face.

After catching my breath, I stood up and gazed down from the summit. The view was breathtaking. The entire Kyoto landscape was in sight. Both high-rise and short buildings all looked so small from up here. You could also see the lush greenery covering the mountain and the seamlessly never-ending trail of orange torii gates stretching from the base to the summit. It was a spectacular sight, and I was captivated by the scenery. "Look, Arima! The sun is setting!" Hikari exclaimed in excitement. The sun was slowly sinking to the horizon, and gradually the burning light of the sun got dull, and the sky turned from blue to reddish-orange. As I was admiring the beauty of the sunset, Hikari grabbed my hand unexpectedly. I was surprised by her actions and turned to Hikari. I was uncertain if it was the tint from the reddish sky or if Hikari was blushing.

"I'm glad I managed to see the sunset with you at the end. Remember the time we first met, and all the outrageous requests I forced you to do together, we had fun, didn't we?" asked Hikari.

Flashbacks of the times I spent with Hikari, the day we met, the cosplay events and the trip came to me. "Yes… It was fun. I tried a lot of new things thanks to you!" I replied.

Hikari then grabbed my shoulders and leaned in for a kiss. A tear rolled down her right cheek. Hikari looked at me with sadness in her eyes and said: "Arima, thank you for all the things you have done for me! I'm sorry I'll be gone before you! My… My final wish is for you to forget about me. Promise me,

Arima!"

I could sense the pain in her voice. There was a spur of emotions building within me. In a moment of impulse, I hugged Hikari tightly.

"You know you are asking the impossible, right? Meeting you gave me meaning in life! The time we spent together is not something I can toss aside and forget!"

Hikari responded with a quavering voice: "It hurts me too! But this is for the best."

I was not willing to let go. I plucked up my courage and declared my innermost thoughts: "Hikari, I love you! I don't want to lose you! No! I am afraid of losing you! Please... Please don't leave me! Whether months or even days, I would like to spend them with you!"

Hikari gently pushed me away and said: "I'm sorry, Arima. I'm not worthy of your emotions. You'll find someone who loves you more than I do."

"No! I want no one else but you!" I expressed, clinging onto Hikari's hand.

Hikari pulled her hand away from me. She then turned her back towards me and left the summit with tears in her eyes.

My heart broke into many pieces. I felt broken on the inside. I could not comprehend the emotions that were running through me and stood there in silence. Feelings blossomed into a relationship that was not to be. I whispered to the heavens: "Why would the heavens play such a joke on us?" Soon, the last tinge of redness in the sky disappeared. It was like nature's farewell kiss for the night. The sky darkened, and the moon appeared above the horizon.

CHAPTER 13:
THE ACCIDENT

I laid on my back and looked up to the night sky while trying to internalise everything that occurred. A sudden thought came to me; images of Hikari's swelling feet appeared in my mind. I thought to myself: "Hikari was in tremendous pain, and it is getting dark. Will she be able to make it down the trail safely?" The fear that Hikari could be in danger or in pain snapped me back into reality. There was nothing more important than ensuring Hikari's safety. I immediately stood up and ran in the direction Hikari went previously.

"Please be safe, Hikari!" I kept muttering these words to myself over and over again in an endless loop. I kept running and searching, but Hikari was nowhere to be found. "She could not have gotten that far!" I thought to myself. Time continued to pass by, and with no signs of Hikari, I felt a sense of rising trepidation. I began shouting for Hikari like a mad man: "Hikari! Where are you? Please answer me!" There was nothing but silence. I kept calling out and running down the hiking trail. Suddenly, I tripped on something and seemingly rolled down a slope.

"Ah!" I shouted in pain. I slowly opened my eyes to see where I was, but my surroundings were pitch black. I tried to reach out for my mobile phone in my bag using my left hand. As I tried to move my left hand to reach for my mobile phone, I was overcome by a stabbing pain similar to that of drilling on my left shoulder. "I think I dislocated my shoulder," I thought to myself. I slowly lifted myself up to an upright position using my right hand and dragged myself to a nearby tree to lean on. I proceeded to reach for my mobile phone using my right hand.

After much difficulty, I finally managed to obtain my mobile phone. I clicked on the ON button, and thankfully my phone was functional. Seeing that the phone was working, I heaved a sigh of relief.

Despite being in pain, the only thought on my mind was Hikari. I decided to give Hikari a call.

"Will Hikari answer my call?" I pondered.

"Eh! Is that the sound of a ringtone?" I could hear a faint sound which sounded like a ringtone.

I clung tightly to the bulk of the tree that I was leaning on and pulled myself up with all my might. After many numerous failed attempts, I eventually managed to get back on my feet. It was hard seeing the path ahead, so I turned on the flashlight on my mobile phone to help me see better. I proceeded to trace the sound of the ringtone. The sound of the ringtone slowly crescendoed. I shone my flashlight in front, and there was a body laying motionlessly in front of me.

I freaked out and immediately switch off the flashlight of my mobile phone. I gulped a mouthful of my saliva. "Is that a dead body?" My hands started to tremble as I was overwhelmed by fear. I eventually braced myself and shone the flashlight to the front again. I caught a glimpse of the clothes on the body.

It seemed to have a flower pattern. Images of Hikari wearing a flower pattern yukata appeared in my mind. My legs turned soft. "Please do not be Hikari!" I prayed as I slowly approached the body.

My worst fear had turned into reality. Laying there motionless was Hikari. I dropped to the ground and lost grip of my mobile phone. I was petrified. I did not know what to do. Slowly, I braced myself and gently shook Hikari. But there was no reaction. "Hikari… Hikari! Stop pretending! Wake up! Please wake up!" I called, but Hikari laid completely still. Seeing that Hikari remained unconscious, I cried: "Hikari! I beg you! Please wake up!" I screamed at the top of my lungs: "Help! Help! Someone, please help!"

Thoughts of regret filled me: "If only I ran after her immediately. None of this would have happened!" Tears continued rolling down my cheeks uncontrollably. I could not help but blame myself: "I was the one who caused this!" I clenched my fist and punched the ground as hard as I could. Despite being injured, the emotional pain I felt was more intense than my external injuries.

Suddenly, I heard a faint breathing sound

emitting from Hikari. I quickly leaned my ear towards Hikari's face and noticed that she was still breathing, but it was shallow. "Hikari is alive! I need to call for help! I need to call for help!" I scrambled to find my phone. I immediately called the rescue team hotline. "My friend is unconscious! We are stuck! Please help us!" I wailed.

The operator tried calming me down. "Where is your location?" The operator enquired.

"I... I fell down a slope som...somewhere in the middle of the Fu... Fushimi Inari hiking trail!" I said stammering.

The operator then assured me: "Don't worry! We will send a rescue team to locate you as soon as possible!"

She proceeded to ask about Hikari's condition. I explained to the operator that Hikari was unconscious, and her breathing was getting weaker by the minute. The operator reassured me that the rescue team would arrive soon. She also told me to monitor Hikari's breathing and perform CPR on her if necessary. Subsequently, we ended the call as she advised me to conserve my phone's battery in case of any further emergencies.

I sat beside Hikari in silence, looking at Hikari laying unconsciously on the ground.

"What if I did not agree to go on this trip?"

"What if I had not said yes back then?"

"What if the hospital encounter did not occur?"

"Would this have happened?"

"No, surely none of this would have happened. It's all my fault, it was me who chose to oblige her! It was me who caused this!"

I felt so helpless in this situation. There was nothing I could do but pray that the rescue team would arrive as soon as possible. Humans are so pathetic. When we are incapable of doing anything, the only thing we can do is pray for the best. "Please hang in there, Hikari!" I muttered.

Twenty-five minutes later, I could hear shouts which appeared to be from the rescue team. "We are here!" I shouted. The rescue team expressed that they could hear my voice but could not identify my exact position. I went on to set the flashlight of my mobile to blinking mode, attempting to signal the attention of the rescue team. Seeing the blinking lights, the rescue team managed to locate us. One of the rescue members attached himself to a safety harness and lowered to our location.

"Are you injured?" asked the rescue team member.

"I'm fine! Please…save her! She is extremely important to me." I begged.

The rescue member slowly carried her onto a stretcher, and with the help of the other members, she was slowly lifted to the hiking trail platform. Hikari was given immediate medical attention to stabilise her condition and was quickly sent to the nearest hospital. I was rescued shortly after and was also sent to the same hospital for treatment. The entire time, my mind was constantly filled with worry about Hikari's condition.

CHAPTER 14:
WORSENING CONDITION

The duration from Fushimi Inari Taisha to the hospital was a five-minute drive. Soon I arrived at the hospital and was attended to by a nurse from the accident and emergency department. Hikari was nowhere to be seen.

"How is Hikari? Is she in any form of danger?" I asked the nurse who was attending to my wounds.

"Are you referring to the girl that arrived before you?" asked the nurse.

I stood up and said in agitation: "Yes! She's the one I'm referring to! How is she?"

"Please stop fidgeting!" The nurse requested.

"Please tell me about her condition!" I pleaded.

"Sir, please calm down… I'm not sure about her exact condition. From what I heard, she's not doing too well. The doctors are trying their best to treat her," said the nurse.

Hearing the news that Hikari was not doing well, my mind went blank. I lost my composure completely. "Please let me see her! I'm fine!" I pleaded. Blood was oozing out of my cuts.

"Please calm down! You are in no position to walk around! Your wounds must be attended to immediately!" insisted the nurse.

The words that came out of the nurse's mouth were nothing but noise to me. My mind was fixated only on one thing, Hikari. I was adamant about seeing Hikari. The nurse proceeded to grab my arm, attempting to restrain me, but I broke from her grip instantly and walked towards the door. The nurse shouted across to another nurse: "Go get a doctor! HURRY!" The other nurse zoomed off to call for help. "Patient Arima! Please stop moving around!" exclaimed the nurse.

Just as I managed to reach the door, a doctor walked in.

The doctor introduced: "I am Dr Hiroshi. I'm part of the team of doctors who are treating Hikari."

Upon hearing that, I instinctively held onto the arm of the doctor using my right hand. "How is Hikari's condition?" I asked.

"Before I tell you about Hikari's condition, I would like you to calm down and allow the nurse to attend to your wounds." requested Dr Hiroshi.

Dr Hiroshi was insistent that I was treated first, or he would not inform me of Hikari's condition. Understanding the circumstance, I acceded to his request and allowed the nurse to attend to my wounds. The pain I was experiencing throughout my body was intensifying. Perhaps it was due to the adrenaline effect wearing off.

"Ouch!" I exclaimed as the nurse applied an antiseptic to my wounds.

"Now you feel pain, huh?" ridiculed the nurse. I felt too embarrassed to even reply.

I prevented myself from emitting any noise as it would further embarrass me. The pain was immense. I clenched my right fist tightly and gritted my teeth.

After a torturous fifteen minutes, "It's finished!" noted the nurse.

"Phew!" I let out a sigh of relief. "Finally, it is over!" I thought to myself.

I thanked the nurse for treating me and apologised for my behaviour earlier. I then turned to the Dr Hiroshi, who was waiting patiently at a corner for the nurse to finish treating my wounds.

"Can you tell me about Hikari's condition?" I enquired.

"Okay, now then. First, promise me that you will remain calm regardless of what I am about to say." Dr Hiroshi sought my understanding.

I closed my eyes and took a deep breath before releasing it slowly to compose myself. Gradually, I opened my eyes and proceeded to look into the Dr Hiroshi's eyes. "I'm ready for the news," I said with certainty.

"Hikari is currently still unconscious and put under close observation. Her external injuries were not severe and have already been treated but what she is suffering from is internal. But please be mentally prepared," informed Dr Hiroshi.

Dr Hiroshi further noted to me the ward Hikari was admitted to, and that Hikari's parents were making their way to the hospital. Dr Hiroshi gently patted my back and left the room with the nurse. The door was shut, and I was left alone in the room. I was dumbfounded. Even without the doctor telling me the exact details of Hikari's condition, the connotation of his words was crystal clear to me.

When I was a kid, I had the warmth and the love of my parents. They were my everything, and I lost them both at once due to the accident. I've shut myself up ever since. Only after meeting Hikari, did I regain laughter and enjoyment in life. She brought me out of that dark place. But now, I would have to lose her. Everything was repeating itself once again.

I spoke under my breath grudgingly: "It's really unfair. I always seem to draw the short end of the straw. First my parents and now Hikari…"

A teardrop fell from my right eye, and soon tears were pouring down uncontrollably. Words could not express my devastation and the complexity of my feelings. My heart felt like it was pierced by thousands of thorns. Tears continued to fall till every last tear dried up and I sat there in silence.

"Hikari's parents should be coming soon. I cannot see them looking like this." I told myself and went to grab some tissues from the desk in the room to wipe my tears before changing to a fresh set of clothes to look more presentable. I stared at my reflection in the mirror located in the room and forced a smile, despite feeling devastated. After I was fully composed, I exited the room and headed to Hikari's ward.

CHAPTER 15:
THE LETTER

I waited patiently for Hikari's parents outside Hikari's ward as I lacked the courage to enter due to the guilt I was experiencing. I simply peered through the glass panel of the door to see Hikari. Hikari laid on the hospital bed motionlessly with a breathing tube inserted through her mouth. It was a painful sight to see Hikari in that condition. The more I saw her in that state, the more the feeling of despair and regret built within me. I could not help but feel responsible for the condition Hikari was in.

Seeing Hikari in that condition triggered flashbacks of my parents. They were laying motionlessly on hospital beds. They also had breathing tubes inserted into them, and within days they were both laying in coffins, one after another. Images of me crying and calling out to them without getting a response remerged from my mind.

"Sorry, are you Arima?"

I snapped back to reality upon being called. A woman with blonde hair who looked like a foreigner approached me. "Yes… Yes! May I know you are…?" I asked.

"I am Hikari's mother. Nice to meet you."

Realising the woman standing in front of me was Hikari's mother, I immediately knelt on the ground and bowed my head to the floor. "I'm sorry. I'm aware that no matter what I say, it would mean nothing. I'm not asking for your forgiveness, but apologising is all I can do now." I expressed with remorse.

Hikari's mother knelt down and slowly lifted my head with her gentle hands. She proceeded to give me a hug and patted my shoulder. "It's not your fault… I was aware that this day would eventually come due to her condition. Don't blame yourself." Hikari's mother comforted me.

"But if I did not go on this trip with her… This would not have happened! We even kept this trip from you!" I cried.

"No! Hikari's father and I were fully aware that she was with you throughout this trip. Yue was worried and informed us about this trip the night before Hikari left, but we still wanted her to go despite being worried about her condition. Hikari told us many wonderful things about you. She said that she could feel like herself again when she was with you. You brought joy to her once again, and I'm sure she enjoyed every moment with you! Thank you for getting along with Hikari!" Hikari's mother expressed with gratitude.

"No, I'm the one who should be grateful to Hikari! She helped me more than I helped her!" I said in response.

"I'm glad both of you were happy!" She let out a smile.

Hikari's mother helped me to my feet and dusted my knees with her hands. She then reached for her bag.

"Here… Hikari asked me to give this to you

when she is gone but I thought you should have it now."

It was a letter. I politely accepted the letter from her. Hikari's mother then reached for her bag again.

"I found this box in the kinchaku that she was carrying, which I think was meant for you." Hikari's mother handed a wooden box over to me and proceeded to see Hikari in her ward.

I searched for a seat in a quiet corner, and carefully opened the letter to read its contents. It was a handwritten letter.

Hi Arima,

If you're reading this, I must be gone. I'm sure you're feeling a great sense of relief that you are finally free from me.

Remember the time when you first learned of my secret more than two months ago? Time flies, doesn't it? Though it was a short time, it really felt much longer. Truth is, even before our encounter in the hospital, I had a little crush on you, but you were so unapproachable and cold towards everyone. So, when you knew my secret, I took the opportunity to get closer to you and I'm glad I did.

The time I spent with you was short, but it was the most memorable time of my life and I hope it was for you too.

I know Yue will be devasted when she gets the news, and she will probably hate you for not letting her in on it. Sorry for making you keep such a big secret. I really hope that my two best friends will be able to continue on together without me. Yue may look tough on the outside, but she is actually soft and warm on the inside. Please take care of her in my stead. But I will leave that to you since I would have used up all my three wishes by now. So if you both want to part ways, that will be fine with me too. I just want the both of you to be happy.

I am coming to the end of my letter now. I hope you live your life with smiles and laughter. Do remember me occasionally and water the flowers on my grave. Thanks for obliging me and thanks for learning my secret.

(Empty Space of the Letter)

Remember to smile and not grieve too much about me,

Love,

Hikari

"Can I really learn to smile again, without you around?" I questioned myself.

I proceeded to open the wooden box, which was found in the kinchaku Hikari was carrying. It contained two bracelets. They were two red braided cord bracelets, one with gold inari fox and the other with a silver inari fox. Engraved within the wooden box was a sentence. "Couples who wear these bracelets shall never be apart even in death." There was also a small note left by Hikari which read: "This is a gift from me. There are two bracelets. One is for you and the other is for your future soulmate. I sincerely pray that you will meet the owner of the other bracelet."

"My soulmate… Hikari, you are the person I truly want to be with," I mumbled under my breath.

As I was still drowning in sorrow, I noticed a

gap between her signing off the letter and the final paragraph of the letter. I touched the empty space, and I could feel markings near the blank space of the letter. It felt like it had been erased. I quickly ran to the counter to borrow the pencil and shaded the empty portion of the letter. Words started to uncover from the blank space of the letter. The words read:

I have been lying all along. I'm actually afraid of dying, and I do not want to die. Meeting you, made me more afraid of losing you. Time and time again, you made my heart flutter. Remember in school, when others thought we were a couple, I was actually secretly very happy. My heart pounded rapidly but I did not push our relationship further as I was aware I was dying soon. If I was given one wish, I wished I did not have this disease and had more time to be with you. I love you, Arima. But I will be gone soon, and there is nothing I can do. I feel so helpless...

After seeing the hidden part of the letter, I felt a sharp pain pierce through my heart, but I had no more tears left to cry. I felt so helpless and pathetic. More than anything, I want to be with Hikari, but there was nothing I can do.

Suddenly, I recalled the words of the white fox.

"Soon, we'll meet again, and when that time comes, I'd love to see the decision you will make."

Those were the words the white fox said to me before I blacked out. Recalling the words of the white fox, I immediately stood up and was prepared to take on the hiking trail of Fushimi Inari Taisha again. But there was something I had to do first.

I took a deep breath and opened the door of Hikari's room. Hikari's parents were sitting beside her. I requested: "Sorry… Do you mind if I can spend some time in private with Hikari?" Hikari's parents were understanding and exited the room, leaving me alone with Hikari.

I placed a bouquet of tulips on the table near Hikari's bed and sat beside her. "Hi Hikari, it's me, Arima. I'm sorry… I'm late. I was afraid and did not have the courage to enter your room until now. You would usually tease me by now. I really hope to see you get up and tease me again. I saw the part of the letter you erased, and this is my answer to you!" I proceeded to take the bracelet with the gold inari fox and tied it on her right wrist with one hand as my left shoulder was dislocated. "Hikari, I want the owner of the other bracelet to be you. I love you! I'm not letting you go! I'm already filled with scars and having more would not matter. This time I will not give up on you! Not only in this lifetime, but also in the next, I want you to be my soulmate! No matter how many cycles of reincarnation it takes, I'll be waiting for you!" I cried my heart out.

Hikari let out a teardrop in her left eye. I proceeded to tie the other silver bracelet on my left wrist and said: "Now we are together and will never be apart!" I left the wooden box on the table beside her bed and gently leaned forward to kiss Hikari on her forehead.

I took another glance at Hikari before leaving the room. I told myself: "No matter what it takes, never again would I lose a loved one!"

CHAPTER 16:
THE DECISION

By the time I left the hospital, it was already the middle of the night, approximately 2am and darkness filled the sky. The sky was darker than obsidian, which enhanced the brightness of the pale crescent moon. All public transportations were halted at this time of the night. The roads were empty with no signs of cars or buses, and silence filled the night. The silence was occasionally disrupted by the wavering cries of owls. The paths, however, were covered by bright streetlamps. The duration from the hospital to Fushimi Inari Taisha was approximately twenty minutes by foot. I walked with long strides to reach the shrine as fast as possible. Slowly the strides escalated to running, and I arrived at the entrance of Fushimi Inari Taisha in ten minutes instead of the usual twenty minutes.

"Huff! Huff!" I breathe heavily. I braced and told myself: "This is not the time to be tired. Hikari is waiting for me!"

The hiking trail was lit up with lanterns and traditional-looking lamps. I jolted up the trail with all my might, searching for the intersection. "It should be here somewhere!" I thought to myself. But the intersection was nowhere to be found. "Maybe I missed it!" I muttered to myself and proceeded to hike down. This process went on repeatedly, and I was drenched in sweat after the numerous attempts. I shouted: "Old lady! Where are you? Lead me to that path again!" But only silence greeted me. "White fox! Show yourself!" I yelled, but there was nothing but silence. "Tell me! What do you want me to do to allow me to see you again?" I screamed. If anyone was there at that time, I would probably be sent to the mental institute. But thankfully, I was alone. Despite my cries, there was nothing but the echo of my calls. My legs started to give way, and I knelt down on the ground. My body was on the verge of breaking due to the strain I put myself through despite my injury. I told myself: "Arima, you cannot collapse now! You promised yourself, didn't you?" My vision was getting cloudy, the exhaustion in my body was too overwhelming, and I collapsed to the ground.

"Wake up! Arima! Wake up!" I heard Hikari's voice, which awoken me.

"Hikari!" I shouted, but no one was beside me. Everything around me was pitch black.

"Where am I?" I asked myself.

A voice came from the winds and said: "You are finally awake."

"This voice! I recognised this voice! It's the voice of that white fox!" I figured. I called out: "White fox! Show yourself!"

A gust of wind blew, and somehow the lanterns around me lit up. I looked around and realised I was at the old shrine. Then the white fox appeared before me and spoke: "Arima, we meet again."

I knelt down and beseeched the white fox: "Mighty white fox! Please heal Hikari and cure her of cancer!"

The white fox feigned ignorance: "Huh? What are you talking about? What makes you think I have the power to save her?"

I begged: "Please… I am willing to do anything! Please save Hikari!"

The white fox grinned with a cunning look: "Anything? Really… Anything? Ah… I have an idea! How about your life for the girl's life? Isn't it fair?"

Many thoughts flashed through my mind. But ultimately, after deliberating, I came to a conclusion.

"So, what's your decision, Arima? It's okay to say no since all humans are afraid of dying. Why would you even give up your life for someone you knew only for a few months," taunted the white fox.

I took a deep breath and looked straight into the eyes of the white fox. "If that is what it takes, I am willing to trade my life for hers," I said firmly.

"Interesting? I never expected such a gesture from you. I thought you only cared about yourself, didn't you?" asked the white fox.

"Yes! I didn't care about anyone else other than myself. But that's before I met her! Hikari is not anyone else! She's precious to me!" I responded.

"I see… You're different now," said the white fox.

"But I have a request; I pray that you will be benevolent and make her forget me and find someone who loves her as much as I do!"

"Wouldn't your sacrifice be meaningless if she forgets you?"

"She doesn't need to know my pain. Me suffering alone is more than enough. Please make her forget about me and find her a good man deserving of her!" I requested sincerely with pain in my voice. Though it was hard for me, I knew that it was for the best. After all, the person left behind often is the one who suffers the most.

Seeing the compassion I had towards Hikari, the white fox agreed to take my life in exchange for hers and promised to erase her memory of us together: "Very well! I shall grant your wish."

A gust of wind blew, and leaves started to dance around my feet and slowly raised to my waist and above my head. Slowly, my feet began to disappear, followed by my thighs. "I guess this is it!

My life is finally coming to an end. I really wanted to spend my life with Hikari, but I'm glad I can do something for her in return." I thought to myself. I closed my eyes and grabbed onto the bracelet on my left wrist.

As my body was dissipating, the white fox showed me a vision, perhaps out of sympathy. It was a vision where Hikari and I spent our lives together before passing away due to old age. We had two beautiful kids, a boy and a girl. The boy had Hikari's blonde hair and facial features that resembled mine, while the girl looked exactly like Hikari, beautiful, elegant and cheeky at times like she was. We had a happy and fulfilling life together. A teardrop fell from my eye, and I let out a smile. I was grateful to the white fox for showing me a glimpse of my deepest desire.

"Thank you for granting my wish and letting me see Hikari smile again." I mouthed the words under my breath.

Soon, my body dissipated fully, and my soul drifted away. My final thoughts were: "Hikari, may you find happiness and be happy always!"

CHAPTER 17:
YOUR NAME

Spring became winter and winter became autumn, then autumn became summer and summer became spring for many cycles. Flowers that bloomed become buds, and buds turned to withered flowers and withered flowers became fully bloomed repeatedly. Time was reverted. The white fox cycled time back to a point where Hikari's tumour was developing and cursed it.

The white fox chanted: "I, Kami Inari, who commands the origin of power. I boldly curse this tumour, begone under the sound of my voice!"

The tumour in Hikari's liver started to corrode and disappear. The tumour was no longer.

Hikari was not diagnosed with cancer, nor was she suffering from liver cancer. The events that played out also changed as I was not there. But she was still the same vibrant and charismatic girl. She went to the same high school and had the same group of friends, including Yue, who deeply cared for her. After Hikari graduated high school, she pursued a degree in teaching and ultimately became a teacher at the high school she enrolled in.

She always wore a red braided cord bracelet with a gold inari fox on her right wrist. One day as she was sitting at the table in a classroom after finishing her final lesson before the spring vacation, Hikari looked at the bracelet and pondered: "It has been a long time since I had this bracelet, but when and where did I actually get it from?" It had been a mystery for years. She eventually decided to research on it. After searching for clues at home, she found a wooden box which supposedly came with the bracelet. Within the box were the engravings. "Couples who wear these bracelets shall never be apart even in death." There was a small brochure in the box which indicated information about the bracelet.

Apparently, the bracelet originated from Fushimi Inari Taisha and came as a pair. Every pair were custom made and had a unique design. Images in the brochure suggested that the two bracelets had a similar design and were red in colour, with the only difference being the colour of the inari fox. One was gold while the other was silver. They represented the sun and the moon or the "yin" and the "yang" respectively. It was a couple bracelet, used to ensure that lovers who wear this bracelet will never be separated from each other even in death, and one can only coexist when the other is present.

Hikari was bewildered. She wondered why she had this bracelet even before entering high school. She had no recollection of even visiting Kyoto let alone Fushimi Inari Taisha. She also did not recall dating anyone throughout the twenty-three years of her life.

To uncover this mystery, Hikari decided to travel to Kyoto to visit Fushimi Inari Taisha. She travelled to Kyoto via a Shinkansen from Tokyo station. As it was a long train ride, Hikari decided to grab a bento before entering the Shinkansen. There was a wide variety of bento to choose from, but she ultimately chose a tonkatsu bento and boarded the Shinkansen. As she was on the train, she ate the bento. It tasted delicious, but despite her appetite, she could only finish half of the bento box, which was unusual as she could usually eat an entire bento easily.

The Shinkansen passed by a row of cherry blossom trees. It was spring, and cherry blossoms bloomed. As she was admiring the beauty of the cherry blossoms from the windows of the Shinkansen, the words: "They are so beautiful, but soon they will wither like me," blurted from her mouth. She was utterly confused as to why she would say that. "What's wrong with me today? I am really not myself." Hikari pondered to herself.

Hours passed, and soon Hikari arrived at Kyoto station. The entire journey was close to three hours and sitting for too long took a toll on her. "Finally!" She exclaimed and inhaled a deep breath. "Sniff! Sniff! Is that the smell of ramen? Nah! It can't be. I am at the arrival area. There's no way I can smell the ramen here!" Hikari convinced herself that it was her nose that was playing tricks on her.

Hikari took an escalator which led her to the ticket gates. To her surprise, there was indeed a ramen stall right in front of the ticket counter. Hikari was dumbfounded and muttered to herself: "I can't believe there is actually ramen here!" Hikari decided to stop at the ramen stall for lunch and ordered a bowl of Kyoto ramen. As she slurped the noodles, she was bewildered by the taste. The taste of the noodles felt familiar, even though she was sure that it was her first time in Kyoto. She subsequently took the local train to Inari station.

As she walked towards Fushimi Inari Tashi, there were several shops. Most of the shops were newly renovated and had a more modern design. There was a shop in particular that had a traditional appearance. It was a shop renting yukata. Intrigued by the shop design, Hikari decided to enter the shop to browse through the yukatas the shop had to offer while admiring the traditional architecture of the shop.

There was a whole array of yukatas to choose from. Among the many different yukata designs, a particular yukata caught her eye. It was a light pink yukata with white lilies. It had a relatively simple design compared to the selection available, but it seemed to appeal to her. As she dawned upon the yukata and looked at herself in the mirror, a glimpse of an image of her and an unknown boy in a grey yukata with a striped design emerged from her mind. She could not decipher who that person was as his face was covered in shadows.

Hikari walked towards the entrance of the shrine and headed to the honden. The ringing of the bells by people praying at the honden sparked another image in her mind. It was an image of her and the boy praying fervently in front of the honden. "Who is that?" Hikari thought to herself. After saying her prayers to Kami Inari, Hikari proceeded to hike up to the summit of the shrine.

Throughout the trip, everything felt like it had happened before. Like déjà vu. From the taste of the bento to the cherry blossom trees to the ramen stall, the yukata and the honden all felt like things she had experienced before. Hikari was baffled by the situation and kept replaying the events in her mind as she hiked up the trail.

By the time she reached the summit, the sun was about to set. She stared at the crimson red sky. As she was admiring the beauty of the sunset, she noticed tears rolling down her cheeks. She was bewildered and was unsure why she was crying. As the sun slowly sets, she felt extreme pain and sorrow overwhelming her. Tears flowed down uncontrollably, and she was in despair. She knelt down and grabbed the bracelet on her wrist tightly. She was unsure of the burst of emotions she was feeling, why she was crying and why she felt such sorrow within her.

Suddenly, a hand holding a handkerchief appear in front of her.

"Here! Take this!" The stranger said.

Hikari was taken aback and tried to regain her composure to prevent further embarrassment. "It's okay! Thanks for the offer, but I am fine!" Hikari replied in a hoarse voice.

"Take it! I insist!"

"Okay… Thank you."

Just as Hikari was about to take the

handkerchief from the stranger, she noticed a bracelet on the stranger's wrist that was identical to the one she saw in the brochure.

Being caught in the moment, Hikari grabbed the stranger's wrist and asked: "Where…Where did you get this bracelet?"

The stranger replied: "I had it for a very long time. It was a gift from a girl a long time ago."

Hikari looked up towards the stranger, and shadows of the image of the guy she had in her visions slowly uncovered. The man in front of her was the person in the images she saw. Her eyes gleamed in joy, and tears continued to flow down her cheek.

"May… May I know your name? I am Mori Hikari!"

The stranger replied: "My name is Arima! Takashi Arima! Nice to meet you!"

The pair shook each other hands and broke out a smile.

---- The End ---